11-13

Author:
Jacqueline Morley studied English at Oxford University. She has taught English and History, and now works as a freelance writer. She has written historical fiction and nonfiction for children.

Additional artists:
Mark Bergin, Giovanni Caselli, John James, David Stewart, Gerald Wood

Series creator:
David Salariya was born in Dundee, Scotland. He has illustrated a wide range of books and has created and designed many new series for publishers in the UK and overseas. David established The Salariya Book Company in 1989. He lives in Brighton, England, with his wife, illustrator Shirley Willis, and their son Jonathan.

Editor: **Jamie Pitman**

Editorial Assistant: **Rob Walker**

This edition first published in 2014 by Book House

Distributed by Black Rabbit Books
P.O. Box 3263
Mankato
Minnesota MN 56002

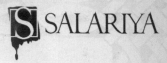

© 2014 The Salariya Book Company Ltd

Printed in the United States of America.
Printed on paper from sustainable forests.

Cataloging-in-Publication Data is available from the Library of Congress

ISBN: 978-1-908973-93-1

Ex Libris

World of Myths & Legends

Written by
Jacqueline Morley

Illustrated by
Carolyn Scrace

Created and designed by
David Salariya

Contents

A World of Myths & Legends

This map shows the origins of a selection of the stories in this book.

1. Raven is a typical Native American "trickster" hero, both mischievous and helpful, animal and human.

2. From the Nez Perce of the northwestern plateau of North America comes the tale of Beaver who brought people the gift of fire.

3. The New Mexican Zuni tell of a monster who ate the clouds.

4. The Aztecs of Mexico had a story about the King of the Dead.

5. The Urubu of the Amazon basin in Brazil know how the moon was made.

6. From Peru comes the tale of a llama who knew that a great flood was coming.

7. According to Irish legend, the Demon of the Lake was not as savage as he seemed at first.

8. King Arthur is the hero of a British legend that originates from Celtic traditions.

9. In the Norse mythology of northern Europe, Queen Hel ruled the underworld.

10. The unicorn was believed to actually exist and was a symbol of purity to medieval Christians across central and eastern Europe.

11. The Minotaur of Crete is just one of the amazing monsters that appear in ancient Greek myths.

12. From ancient Mesopotamia comes the story of the she-monster Tiamat.

13. The ancient Egyptian god Osiris was killed and came back to life again.

14. Anansi the spider man was so well loved that West Africans took his stories with them to the Caribbean.

15. The Nigerians have their own unique version of how the world was made.

16. Prince Rustam was a hero of Persian legend who fought off a dragon with his faithful horse Rakhsh.

17. This fish is the Hindu god Vishnu in one of the many shapes he took to help the world.

18. From China comes the story of Yi, the Great Archer, who saved the world from being burned to a cinder.

19. When the Japanese goddess Izanami died, her husband tried to bring her back from the dead.

20. The native people of Australia tell countless stories of their Dreamtime.

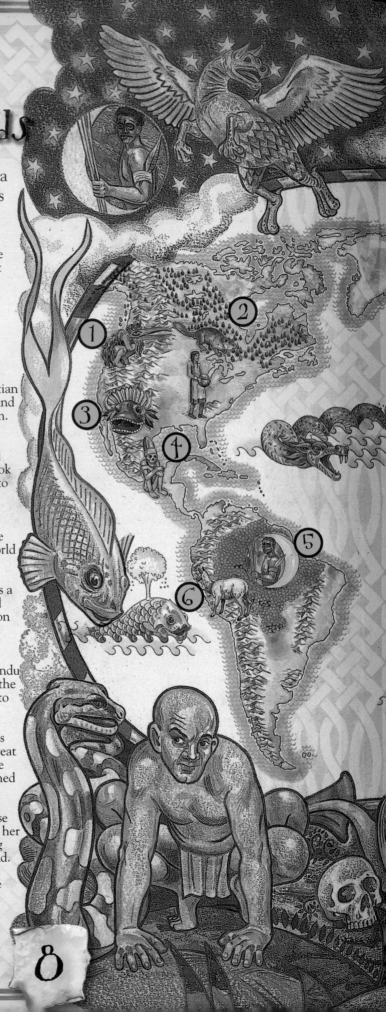

Introduction

The stories in this book are very old—so old that it is impossible to say who first created them. They come from all over the world and in their homelands these tales have been told and retold so many times it seems they have always existed.

The stories often originated from people living much closer to nature than most of the world does now. Those early men and women—our ancestors—believed the earth, the sun, the moon, and stars were gods, or if they were not, gods had placed them in the sky. They asked themselves what sort of beings these gods could be, how they had made the world and why. How had the first men and women been created and what happened to people when they died?

The answers to these questions took the shape of stories and were taught by one generation to the next. These ancient "explanation" tales are called myths. Myths tell of events that couldn't be explained any other way and tend to include supernatural beings—gods, goddesses, and unearthly powers.

The stories take place outside the normal, earthly concept of time and rarely refer to actual historical events. Legends are slightly different because they tell of "long ago"—a time when monsters were common and heroes walked the earth. Whether they are myths or legends, these stories are worth retelling once again.

Heracles and the Hydra

The mythical Greek hero Heracles had to perform twelve tasks after unwittingly committing a grisly murder. His second task was to defeat the Lernean Hydra, a vicious nine-headed water beast.

Myths of creation

How did the world begin? Most mythologies tell that before anything else existed there was a "first being" who made the world. With no world in which to set the story and only one character, often such myths do not have a lot to say about him (or her). It is when the first being creates other gods that things really begin to happen.

The ancient Egyptians believed that Ra the creator made Shu and Tefnut, the gods of air and moisture, and these in turn were the parents of Nut, the sky, and Geb, the earth. But Ra was in love with the sky goddess and was angry when he saw how closely the earth embraced her. He ordered Shu to separate them forever and that is why the air holds the sky high above the earth.

The Maoris of New Zealand also say that the first two beings, Rangi and his wife Papa, hugged each other so tightly that when their sons were born they could not get out from between their parents. One of the sons began to push his father, Rangi, upward with his feet. He pushed until he was upside down with the effort. His brothers helped him and together they forced their parents apart. Rangi became the sky and Papa the earth. When the rain falls, Rangi is weeping with grief at his separation from Papa.

Rangi and Papa

Detail from an intricately carved decoration in a Maori meeting house. Rangi, the Sky Father, and Papa, the Earth Mother, the first parents of the Maori nation, are shown embracing each other.

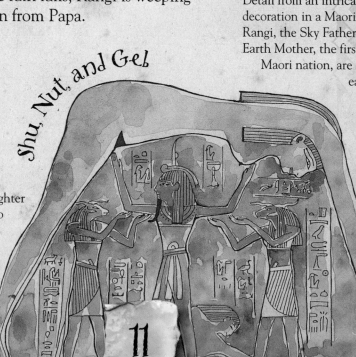

Shu, Nut, and Geb

Shu holds up the body of his daughter Nut to form the arch of the sky so that she can no longer reach her beloved Geb. This picture, based on a painting more than 3,000 years old, shows how the ancient Egyptians imagined the scene.

11

Dreamtime

Spirit ancestors—an Aboriginal myth

The Aboriginal people of Australia believe that the world around them is the creation of their spirit ancestors. These ancestors sleep beneath the earth or in the rocks or trees. In a period called the Dreamtime, the ancestors awoke from their slumber and walked the earth, some as humans, some as animals or plants.

Wherever they went they touched the desert and the rocks and living things took shape beneath their touch. Here and there they found strange unformed lumps lying on the ground.

They made knives of stone and carved these lumps into people, giving them faces, arms, and legs.

Wherever the spirit ancestors passed they left sacred signs upon the landscape, in the shape of a rock, a waterhole, or a tree. Such signs are everywhere, for the Dreamtime and the spirit ancestors are never far away.

It is believed that every human being exists eternally in the Dreamtime, before and after their birth and death. An eternal spirit enters the world through a mother in her fifth month of pregnancy, and returns to the Dreaming after its death as a human.

Australia

There are more than 400 different groups of Aborigines in Australia, and each one tells its mythical stories in a different way. The Australian deserts are vast, flat, and mostly empty, so it is understandable that the huge rocks that dot the landscape of the Australian outback could be seen as the work of spirits.

Traversing the deserts

The spirit ancestors traverse the desert as animal or human, forming human beings from lumps of rock. Spirit ancestors took the forms of many creatures, such as dingoes, kangaroos, and exotic birds and amphibians.

Grapevine

Mandan vine climbers—a North American myth

The Mandan of North America say that, in the beginning, their people lived in an underground world by the shores of a great lake. One day a group of their men was out hunting and came across a mass of gnarled roots hanging down from somewhere far above their heads. They began to climb it. After a long climb they discovered at last that they had scaled the root of an enormous grapevine that was growing in the world above. This world was very pleasant. The sun was shining, the plants were tall and green, and there were animals in every thicket just waiting for huntsmen. The men scrambled down the root and told their families of their wonderful find. The whole of the Mandan people decided to move to the world above.

The tribe set off and began to climb the vine root. It swayed and creaked under their weight but was safe until a very heavy woman insisted on trying to climb up. Her weight broke the root and those who were waiting behind her had to remain in their underground world.

The Mandan in the upper world did not forget their first home completely. Mandan people believe that after they die they will return there to live beside the lake.

Rushing War Eagle

The Mandan are one of the Sioux peoples of the Great Plains. This portrait of a Mandan chief wearing a necklace of bear claws comes from a photograph taken in the 1890s. His name was Rushing War Eagle.

The Mandan's ancestors were said to have climbed the thick roots of a giant grapevine up into our world.

15

The first woman

Pandora's box—a Greek myth

After the world was made the gods created men and women. In many myths, it appears that the creator god felt the world lacked something until it had people in it. Men and women were usually formed together, as companions, but there are several stories that say women were created later—the ancient Greek myth of Pandora, for example.

Zeus, king of the gods, was not pleased with the new race of men that had appeared on Earth. He suspected the men—and one in particular, named Prometheus—of plotting with his enemies the Titans. Zeus wanted revenge. He created the first woman, the beautiful Pandora, and sent her down to Earth. Her name meant "all gifts," for Zeus told the gods to bless her with every charm that could make men love her. Aphrodite, goddess of love, gave her beauty, and Hermes, the gods' messenger, gave her wit and guile.

The moment Prometheus set eyes on Pandora he guessed that Zeus was up to something. He warned his brother, Epimetheus, not to speak to her, but Epimetheus was kind-hearted and took Pandora into his house. She had brought a box with her, a gift from Zeus which he had told her she must never open. But Pandora soon grew bored and longed to look inside, although Epimetheus begged her not to. She waited until his back was turned and lifted the lid of the box.

Immediately, a swarm of hideous creatures shot into the air: envy, sickness and old age, lies, treachery, famine, and war. Pandora shrieked as they flew out into the world, where they have been tormenting people ever since. One tiny creature fluttered after them, and that was hope, the only comfort Zeus allowed humankind.

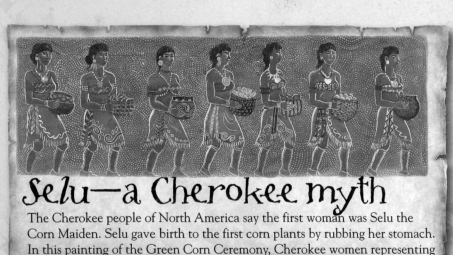

Selu—a Cherokee myth

The Cherokee people of North America say the first woman was Selu the Corn Maiden. Selu gave birth to the first corn plants by rubbing her stomach. In this painting of the Green Corn Ceremony, Cherokee women representing Selu carry baskets containing the first crops of the year.

Pandora

17

Obatala's creation story

Obatala— a Yoruban myth

In the beginning the great god Olorun ruled the sky. Below there was nothing but water, for the world had not yet been made. One day the young god Obatala peered down and thought how dull the water looked. "Something should be done to brighten it up," he thought. So he went to Olorun and asked permission to create land. "You may certainly make land," said Olorun, "if you know how."

Obatala consulted the magician god Orunmila. "You must first make a golden chain, as long as you can," he told him. "Then you must fill a snail shell with sand and put the shell in a bag, together with a white hen, a black cat, and a palm nut. You must climb down the chain with them until you reach the water."

Obatala took the bag, hooked the chain to the edge of the sky, and climbed down. But the chain was not long enough for Obatala to reach the water. "Use the sand in your snail shell!" Orunmila called down from the sky. Obatala emptied the snail shell and the sand made a small dry hillock in the water. "Now free the white hen!" called Orunmila.

Obatala dropped the hen onto the hillock where it immediately began to scratch and scatter sand to the left and to the right. Wherever the sand fell it formed land.

Africa

The Yoruban religion is possibly the largest African-born religion in the world. In Africa, traditional religions like this are now greatly overshadowed by the rise of Christianity in the South and Islam in the North.

Obatala dropped down, dug a hole, and buried his palm nut. At once a palm tree shot up and dropped more nuts which grew into a shady forest on the land. Obatala made himself a house of palm bark and palm leaves. There he lived, with just his cat for company.

Olorun looked down from the sky. "Is all well?" he asked. "Well enough," replied Obatala, "but it is brighter in the sky." So Olorun tossed the sun down to shine on the world.

Finally, Obatala made little figures out of clay and when Olorun breathed life into them they became the first men and women in the world.

Golden chain

Snail shell

Obatala's items

Black cat

White hen

Journeys of the dead

Osiris—an Egyptian myth

Stories of grain gods are widespread. The death or disappearance of grain gods has a negative affect on harvests. Like seeds that seem dead in winter, such gods are often believed to go underground. In their absence the earth is barren and nothing grows. But, like plant seeds, they generally spring back to life again.

Osiris was the grain god of the ancient Egyptians. Long ago, when the gods lived on Earth, Osiris ruled Egypt. He ruled it well, teaching the people to grow crops and vines. But his evil brother Set was jealous of his power and murdered him, nailing his body into a chest and throwing it into the River Nile.

flight of Telepinus

Telepinus, the Hittite god of fruitfulness, rejected the world and vanished into the wilderness. Without him nothing grew and the gods tried everything to find him. Eventually he reappeared, riding on an eagle's back, and brought the world back to life.

The river carried the chest far out to sea. Osiris' sorrowful wife Isis searched the world, until at last she found the chest magically encased in the trunk of a tamarisk tree. She secretly brought it back to Egypt. However, Set found its hiding place, hacked the body of Osiris to pieces, and scattered the bits along the Nile.

Not giving in, Isis built a boat out of papyrus reeds and once again searched the waters until she had found each and every piece. Through magic, prayers, and love, she breathed new life into her beloved Osiris.

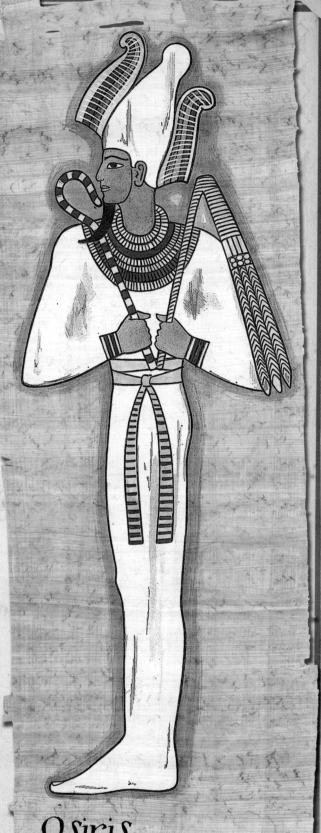

Ancient Egypt

The ancient Egyptians were lucky to live in a rich and prosperous land blessed with hot sun and a good water supply from the River Nile. As they had so much to be thankful for it's no wonder they worshipped the sun in the form of the god Amun Re. Once a year the Nile flooded, leaving behind a layer of rich black mud that fertilized the crops the following year. For this, the Egyptians thanked the flood god Hapy, a bearded god with water-plants sprouting from his head.

Osiris

Osiris was always portrayed wrapped up like a mummy. This was not an image of death but a symbol of rebirth. Mummification preserved the body and this, the ancient Egyptians believed, enabled a person's soul to live after death, as Osiris had done.

Quest for a loved one

Baldur and Loki—a Norse myth

Baldur the beautiful was the best of the gods: the wisest, the kindest, and the gentlest. Everyone loved him, except Loki, an evil god who was the father of monsters. Baldur's mother Frigg made every stick, stone, and living creature in the world swear never to harm him, but she forgot to ask the mistletoe plant. When Loki learned of this he made the plant into a dart and tricked the blind god Hodur into throwing it at Baldur. The gods were stunned by the death of Baldur. His brother, Hermod the Swift, rode for nine months and nine days to Niflheim, the Land of the Dead. There he begged its ruler, Queen Hel, to let Baldur come back from the dead.

Queen Hel and Hermod

The mysterious old woman

Queen Hel was the daughter of Loki. One half of her face was beautiful and the other was cruel and wrinkled. She turned the fair side of her face to Hermod and agreed to make a bargain with the gods. If everything in the world above Niflheim was willing to weep for Baldur, he could return from the dead.

Hermod rode back to the gods in triumph—he did not doubt that every stick, every stone, and every living thing would weep for Baldur the Beautiful. And so they did, all except one old woman who lived alone in a cave. "She is deaf," people said. "She has not heard about Baldur." They shouted at her to weep but she only glared at them. "My name is Dry Eyes," she replied, "and if you think I'll weep for Baldur you are mistaken. Let Hel keep him!" The old woman was Loki himself, who had taken her shape. As Loki had ruined Queen Hel's bargain, Baldur had to remain in the Land of the Dead.

In the underworld

Aeneas—an Ancient Roman myth

Aeneas, the greatest hero of Roman legends, was summoned to the underworld by his dead father in a dream. To learn how to reach the underworld Aeneas consulted the Sibyl, a priestess who lived in the mountains. "First," the Sibyl told him, "you must find a tree with a golden bough and break off the branch. Proserpina, Queen of the Underworld, will demand this gift."

Aeneas was guided to the tree by a pair of doves, and returned with the golden bough. The Sibyl warned Aeneas of the danger ahead and led him deep into her cave. The Earth trembled and a passage to the underworld opened beneath their feet.

The Sibyl brought Aeneas to the banks of the dismal river Acheron, which circled the realm of Pluto, king of the dead. Aeneas saw a multitude of dead souls scrambling to board a ferry boat, while the grim old ferryman named Charon pushed many of them away.

"Why does he take some and not others?" Aeneas asked. "Only the properly buried may enter Pluto's kingdom," the Sibyl replied. "The unburied must wait a hundred years upon this shore."

At the sight of the golden bough Charon begrudgingly took Aeneas and his companion across the river. There, Pluto's three-headed watchdog Cerberus howled at them until the Sybil tossed the dog a drugged cake to silence him.

The golden bough

The Sybil led Aeneas through fields of spirits, where he recognized dead comrades. He heard the bitter reproaches of his former love, the Queen of Carthage, who had been so in love with Aeneas that she had killed herself.

Before long the route divided. To the left was a flaming river and the fortress in which the evil deeds of the dead were punished. To the right the path led to Elysium where heroes, poets, and philosophers strolled and talked. Here, Aeneas was at last greeted by his father, who told him of his future, foretelling his son's triumphs and the founding of Rome.

Aztec underworld

Quetzalcoatl—an Aztec myth

Quetzalcoatl, whose name means "plumed serpent," was an Aztec god in ancient Mexico. He wore a crest of colored feathers from the quetzal bird. Quetzalcoatl decided to give the world a new race of human beings. He went down to Mictlan, the land of the dead, and found Mictlantecuhtli, its lord, seated on a pile of bones.

A tablet showing a relief of the Aztec god Quetzalcoatl.

Quetzalcoatl

"Give me the bones of my father," Quetzalcoatl begged. "Whatever lies here is mine" was the answer.

Eventually, Mictlantecuhtli agreed to let the bones go if Quetzalcoatl could blow into a conch shell, making a great noise, while walking four times around a circle of jade. Quetzalcoatl took the conch and blew with all his strength but no sound came, for the shell was blocked with earth. He asked the worms that lived among the dead to wriggle into the shell and clear the conch shell out. When it was clear, Quetzalcoatl blew the conch and walked around the jade, thus performing the task he was set.

Mictlantecuhtli reluctantly gave Quetzalcoatl the bones, and told his servants to make sure he did not leave with them. The servants covered a pit with branches so that Quetzalcoatl fell into the trap and lay senseless. Birds swooped on the scattered bones and pecked them to dust.

When Quetzalcoatl eventually recovered he scraped up the bone dust as well as he could, moistened it with his own blood, and molded it into a new human race.

Mictlantecuhtli

27

Izanami and Izanagi

A Japanese myth

Izanami and Izanagi stood on the floating bridge of heaven and stirred the ocean with a jeweled spear. The drops that fell from the spear formed an island where they could live happily together. Izanami gave birth to the wind god, the moon god, and the sun goddess. But when she gave birth to the fire god she was so badly burned that she died.

Izanagi traveled to Yomi, the Land of the Dead, to bring his wife back. He heard her voice but could not see her in the darkness. "I cannot return with you," she told him. "Go back and do not look at me."

But Izanagi longed to see his wife, so he set light to a torch. He turned rigid with horror. Izanami's body had begun to rot and maggots were crawling all over her flesh. She was bitterly ashamed to be seen in such a horrific state. She cried out in fury and summoned all the demons of Yomi to destroy her husband.

Izanagi fled, with the demons close behind. When he reached the entrance to the upper world he closed it behind him with an immense boulder. From behind the boulder Izanami's voice screamed to him, "Every day I will cause 1,000 people to die and bring them to this land." "And every day I will cause 1,500 to be born," Izanagi replied, and he returned to the land of the living.

Japan

The two main religions in Japan are Shintoism and Buddhism. Together, they account for around 90% of the population. Shintoism originated in prehistoric Japan, while Buddhism arrived from Korea in the 6th century.

Izanagi and the boulder

fire and flood

Myths of destruction

Earthquakes, volcanoes, and floods—such disasters were thought to be caused by the gods. A flood that covers the world is a very common myth. Often, the people of the world are blamed for displeasing the gods. In a Babylonian myth the gods sent a flood because people on Earth were irritating them by making too much noise. The Hebrew god, Yahweh, found the world had grown incredibly wicked. There was only one man in it worth saving—Noah.

Before Yahweh flooded the world he told Noah to build an ark (a large ship) to house himself, his family, and two of every living thing. After the rain stopped, Yahweh put a rainbow in the sky as a sign that he would never drown creation again.

According to a Chinese tale, it was not long after the world was made that the god of water and the god of fire had a war and nearly ruined it. The god of water summoned all his underwater creatures and went into battle, but his forces could not withstand the fire god's heat. It melted the jellyfish and roasted the rest of his army.

The water god was so furious that he rammed his head against the mountain that held up the sky. The mountain split and fell, making deep gashes in the Earth. Lumps of the sky fell down and water gushed from the cracks in the ground creating an endless sea. It was up to the creator goddess Nu Wa to mend everything.

After 150 days Noah thought the flood waters seemed to be receding. He released a dove from the ark to see if it could find dry land, but it found no place to settle and flew back to him. When he sent the bird out a week later, it returned with an olive twig in its beak. And so Noah knew that somewhere there must be trees showing above the water.

The legend of Atlantis

A flood destroyed the legendary city of Atlantis, so the ancient Greeks believed. It was said that a giant wave swallowed the island. The sea god Poseidon had built the city and given it walls of brass and palaces of gold. The remains lay somewhere at the bottom of the ocean, but no one has ever found them.

The city of Atlantis collapses into the sea

Drowning the world

Matsya the fish—a Hindu myth

Vishnu as Matsya

A holy man named Manu went each morning to pray by the river, pouring its water over his head from a water pot. One day he found he had scooped up a little fish in his pot. "Don't put me back!" the fish pleaded. "If you do, the big fish will swallow me." So the holy man took the little fish home in his pot.

The next day he found the fish had grown and could hardly turn around in the pot. "Please, holy man, find me more room" it begged. So Manu filled a cauldron with water and put the fish in that, but still it grew and still it begged for more room. Next Manu

A relief showing Vishnu as Matsya. Vishnu came to Earth nine times to save humanity. Hindus believe his tenth appearance is yet to come.

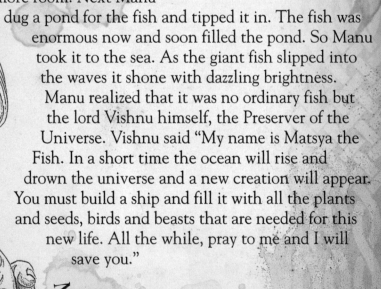

Manu

dug a pond for the fish and tipped it in. The fish was enormous now and soon filled the pond. So Manu took it to the sea. As the giant fish slipped into the waves it shone with dazzling brightness. Manu realized that it was no ordinary fish but the lord Vishnu himself, the Preserver of the Universe. Vishnu said "My name is Matsya the Fish. In a short time the ocean will rise and drown the universe and a new creation will appear. You must build a ship and fill it with all the plants and seeds, birds and beasts that are needed for this new life. All the while, pray to me and I will save you."

Matsya

Manu built the ship as he had been
told and every day he prayed to
Matsya. Then the storm came. The
sea flooded the land and Manu saw
the fish swimming toward him. Its
scales were of shining gold and it
had a golden horn on its head.
It told Manu to throw a rope
around its horn and it towed
the boat to a mountain peak
just above the waters.
Vishnu saved Manu
to be the
father of a
new race.

33

Prometheus

fire from the gods

Prometheus—a Greek myth

For early peoples, fire was a precious possession, providing them with warmth and light. But they knew that if they lost control of it, fire could destroy them. This could be the reason why so many ancient myths describe fire as a power belonging to the gods—humanity was perhaps never meant to have it. All over the world there are tales of how fire was stolen from the gods and given to the people of the Earth.

According to the ancient Greeks, Prometheus the Titan stole fire from heaven for humankind. He smuggled out a small, glowing ember. From this he lit a flaming torch and brought it down from the skies. Zeus punished him with eternal torment in the underworld.

The Fire Giant—a Fijian myth

The people of the Fiji Islands say that a terrible fire giant lived in a cavern in the hills. He had teeth of fire that shot out flames whenever he opened his mouth. The villagers were afraid to go near him, but they had no fire of their own. One night a group of bold men tiptoed into the cave while the giant slept and set fire to a bundle of twigs from his burning breath. The giant leaped up and chased them down the hillside into a small cave, but they blocked the door with a boulder. "I know you have my fire in there!" the giant raged. "Let me take a look."

The men rolled the boulder back a little and the giant thrust his head in. Then they gave the boulder a mighty heave so that it broke his neck against the rocks. The villagers had gained the power of fire and had no further reason to be afraid.

The fire giant

fire from the trees

A North American myth

The Nez Perce people of North America say that long ago, before there were any people in the world, animals and trees walked and talked just as we do. Only the pine trees had the secret of fire, which they would not share.

One winter, it was so cold that the animals almost froze to death. They called a meeting and decided that someone must steal fire from the pine trees.

Starting a fire

This Native American is using a piece of equipment called a fire stick to make fire.

It is easy to see why early peoples believed fire lived in trees. If two pieces of wood are rubbed together in the right way the friction between them produces a spark.

Close to the Grande Ronde River, the pine trees built a great fire to keep themselves warm. But when a hot ember rolled down the bank, Beaver ran off with it. The pine trees chased him along the bank until he took to the water and swam across. The pine trees were tired so they stopped at the river bank. Only the Cedar tree went on chasing Beaver.

Cedar said, "I will run to the top of that hill and see how far ahead he is." Beaver was too far ahead to catch. He gave fire to the willows, the birches, and to many other trees. These trees then shared the secret of fire. Cedar still stands on the top of a hill and there are no other trees anywhere near him because he ran so far ahead of them.

The great archer

A Chinese legend

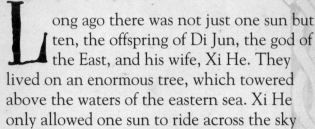

Long ago there was not just one sun but ten, the offspring of Di Jun, the god of the East, and his wife, Xi He. They lived on an enormous tree, which towered above the waters of the eastern sea. Xi He only allowed one sun to ride across the sky each day. Before each dawn Xi He prepared a flying cart and brought it to the top of the tree. The sun of the day bathed, got in the cart, and drove it carefully across the sky, shining just enough to warm the world and make things grow. This duty became very boring and one night the ten suns decided to rebel against their mother.

One morning, before their mother arrived, they all danced into the sky together. The world below felt the heat of all ten suns. The rivers and the seas dried up, the forests shriveled, and the fields caught fire.

Yi, the Great Archer

King Yao saw his people scorched and blinded and sent an urgent message to Xi He. But the ten suns laughed and would not obey their mother.

King Yao summoned Yi, the Great Archer. He gave him ten arrows and ordered him to shoot the suns out of the sky. Yi climbed a rock, took careful aim, and brought one of the suns tumbling down. Its light went out and it fell to the ground as a dead crow. Two, three, four, five, six, seven crows fell, and the heat lessened. As Yi prepared yet another arrow the king cried out.

"Leave us one sun!" he called, but Yi was too far away to hear. He shot the eighth sun and the ninth, but as he reached for the tenth arrow he found his quiver empty. King Yao's swiftest runner had snatched the last arrow. One sun was saved and that is the one that shines in the sky today.

China

The Chinese religions are family-oriented and, unlike Western religions, members can be involved in more than one belief system at a time.

The suns fall as dead crows

Heroes

Legends from around the world

The Bull of Heaven

Gilgamesh

Gilgamesh fights the Bull of Heaven. The goddess Ishtar sent it to ravage Gilgamesh's kingdom because he had enraged her by refusing her love. It was Enkidu who finally tore the bull to pieces, so Ishtar caused him to fall sick and die.

A hero is someone who performs noble deeds and fights for good against evil. The heroes of myths were often related to the gods. Others were shadowy historical figures surrounded by amazing and fantastical legends. An ancient example of this kind of hero is Gilgamesh of Babylon. Gilgamesh was king of Uruk and was a strong but overbearing ruler.

His subjects complained to the gods, who created a wild man called Enkidu to humble him. But after a fierce bout of wrestling, Gilgamesh and Enkidu became firm friends. When Enkidu died, Gilgamesh was left broken-hearted and afraid of death. He decided to consult his immortal ancestor Upnapishtim, to learn how to escape death. To reach his dwelling, Gilgamesh entered the mountain where the sun goes down. Beyond the Sea of Death he came to his friend's home. Upnapishtim gave him no hope. "All things must die," he said, "unless the gods will it otherwise." But Upnapishtim's wife persuaded him to reveal the secret of a plant that grew at the bottom of the ocean. This plant could make the old become young again. Gilgamesh weighted his feet with stones to sink to the sea floor, where he found the miracle plant. But a snake crept up and swallowed it. So Gilgamesh returned to Uruk sad and empty-handed.

The legend of King Arthur is loosely based on a historical figure who fought invaders in the 6th century. Arthur proved himself a true king by pulling the sword Excalibur from a rock. When his leadership of his Knights of the Round Table ended in betrayal and bloodshed, the king was wounded. A ghostly boat took him to the mystical island of Avalon where he remained forever.

King Arthur

The labors of Heracles

A Greek legend

The greatest hero of Greek legend was the champion Heracles. He was amazingly strong. When he was still in his cradle he strangled two serpents, sent by Hera, queen of the gods, to injure Heracles because she hated his mother.

When Heracles grew up, Hera sent him into a fit of madness in which he killed his wife and children. When his madness passed Heracles was in despair at what he had done. He asked the oracle at Delphi what he must do to wipe away his guilt. He was told he must become the servant of his cousin, Eurystheus, and perform ten tasks that he would be set.

Eurystheus was Hera's favorite, a nasty little coward who sent Heracles on the most dangerous errands possible. His first task was to kill a monstrous lion that was devouring the people of Nemea. It could not be harmed by steel or fire so weapons were useless. Instead, Heracles killed it with his bare hands and afterward wore its skin as armor, with its gaping head as his helmet.

Heracles' next task was to kill the Hydra, a many-headed monster that lived in a swamp. When one head was cut off, two would grow in its place.

Heracles threw away his weapons and choked the Nemean lion to death. As no knife could pierce its hide, he used one of the beast's own claws to skin it.

The Hydra

Heracles seared each severed throat with fire, so that new heads could not grow. But Eurystheus did not accept the task as complete because Heracles had help from the chariot driver, who lit the fire. The hero's third task was to kill the ferocious Erymanthian boar. He presented the boar to Eurystheus, who was so scared he hid in a jar and would not come out.

Heracles was then sent to clean the stables of King Augeius, who had such vast herds of cattle that their dung piled up knee-high. The King agreed to give Heracles a tenth of the cattle if he cleared the mess, which he did by knocking down walls and diverting two rivers through the stables. But Eurystheus would not count this labor either, because Heracles had been employed by the King. King Augeius refused to honor his word too.

He said the river god had done the work! In the end, Heracles had to complete two extra labors, twelve in all. Zeus made him immortal as a reward and even Hera became his friend.

Heracles

The Polynesian hero, Maui of a Thousand Tricks, thought the days were too short so he caught the sun in a noose and gave it a beating. Since then it has only been able to limp slowly across the sky, making the days much longer.

Trickster heroes

Raven—a North Pacific legend

Heroes are usually admired for their courage and glorious deeds. But there are quite different types of hero that crop up in stories from many parts of the world. They are the cunning "trickster" heroes who always outwit their opponents and are often up to no good. They are heroes, certainly, because in the tales told about them they always win the day and come out on top. It seems that such trickster figures reflect the rebellious, cheeky side of human nature. In Native American myths, Raven is this type of hero: unpredictable and selfish but sometimes a friend to human beings.

Below, a story is retold from the Tlingit and Haida peoples of the North Pacific Coast about Raven. He brought people light by tricking the great sky chief out of his most prized possession, the sun.

Raven turned himself into a pine-needle and dropped into the stream where the sky chief's daughter was drinking. By swallowing the needle she became pregnant and eventually gave birth to a baby boy, who was Raven in disguise. The baby became a favorite with his grandfather, the sky chief, who let him play with anything he wanted. One day Raven pointed to the box in which the sun was hidden. First his grandfather shut the smoke hole in the roof of the lodge. Then he opened the box.

A Kwakiutl (North Pacific Coast) dancer wears a ritual mask. He is enacting the role of Raven in a religious ceremony.

At once the lodge was flooded with light. The baby rolled the fiery ball of the sun around the floor of the lodge until he seemed bored with it. The sky chief let him have it whenever he asked but always tucked it back in its box afterward.

One day the chief was feeling drowsy and forgot to close the smoke hole when he took out the sun. Raven changed back into his bird shape, seized the sun and flew through the hole into the sky. Seeing some fishermen by the river below he called out "Give me some fish and I will give you light." The fishermen knew Raven was a liar so they laughed at him, but when he lifted his wing and showed them the sun they gave him their fish. Then Raven threw the sun up into the sky for everyone to enjoy.

Anansi and the python

A legend of the Caribbean and of Africa

Anansi was both a spider and a man and is the hero of many tales, like this one from West Africa and the Caribbean. Some villagers were in despair about a giant python that was preying on their children and animals. They went to God to beg for advice. "You had better ask Anansi to help you." said God. "He is always boasting how wise he is. If he can't get rid of the python I shall punish him for boasting. But if he can, I will grant him even greater wisdom."

Anansi took a dish of mashed yams, palm oil, and eggs and put it near the python's hole. When the python came out to eat, Anansi spoke to it politely and admired its length. "You must be as long as the trunk of that tree over there."

"Longer," smirked the python.

"Let's measure you," said Anansi. Anansi cut the tree down with his ax and the python laid itself alongside. He was not quite as long as its trunk. "If I lash your tail to one end and you give a good pull, I'm sure you can stretch the extra bit," said Anansi. The python let himself be tied at the bottom and, while he was concentrating on stretching, Anansi tied him at the top as well. He then chopped the snake into pieces.

Anansi boasted so much about his triumph that God hurled a pot of wisdom at him. It hit Anansi in the middle and nearly split him in two, which is why all spiders have such narrow waists.

The Caribbean

The main religion found throughout the islands of the Caribbean today is Christianity. Although it is the dominant faith, there are many different adaptations in different areas. Recently Caribbean natives have formed their own religion, Rastafarianism, which is Christianity with a distinctly Caribbean style.

Anansi measures the Python

The demon of the lake

An Irish myth

There was once a lord of Ulster named Briccriu of the Poisoned Tongue. He held a feast to which he invited King Conor of Ulster and all his heroes of the Red Branch. He also invited the bravest of them all, Cuchulain, the Hound of Ulster. After a while, Briccriu provoked a quarrel among them as to who was the greatest champion of all Ireland. It was agreed that the choice was among Cuchulain, Conall of the Victories, and Laery the Triumphant.

"The only creature fit to judge among them is the demon of the lake," Briccriu declared, so the demon was summoned from the water. The demon strode into the hall carrying a huge ax, which he offered to the three contestants and proposed a test of courage.

"Any one of you may cut off my head today," he said, "but the same one must let me have a stroke at his neck tomorrow."

Celtic ornament

Ireland

For many centuries, Celtic myths and legends were memorized and passed on by word of mouth, from generation to generation. But, after around AD 500, Christian monks in Celtic lands began to collect these ancient stories and write them down. For reasons still unknown today, the first texts have all vanished, but later copies survive dating from around AD 1200. Thanks to them, we can still enjoy Celtic myths today.

Cuchulain

48

Conall and Laery withdrew from the test, but
Cuchulain took the ax and struck the demon's
head from its body. The demon picked up his
bleeding head, took his ax, and returned to
the lake. The next day he reappeared, quite
whole again, to claim his half of the
bargain. Cuchulain knelt and put his head
on the block, trying to hide his fear. The
demon swung the ax in the air and brought
the blade down... onto the wood of the
block. He told Cuchulain to rise,
the bravest champion of
all Ireland.

Demon of the lake

Monsters good and evil

The Unicorn Horn—a medieval myth

A monster is a creature unknown in the natural world, often an amazing being made up of various parts—the head, or heads, of one beast, the body of another—parts that nature never intended to go together. In the world of myths and legends monsters appear everywhere: the Anglo-Saxon hero Beowulf fought Grendel, a bloodthirsty water monster; the native North Americans dread Windigo, the ice monster that devours solitary hunters; in Fiji, people fear the Ngendei, a being that is half snake, half rock.

Not all monsters are bad. One of the most appealing monsters is the unicorn. In the Middle Ages the unicorn was a symbol of purity. It was believed that unicorns could only be tamed by a pure young girl.

Greeks and Romans described the unicorn as an antelope or wild ass with a long, sharp horn on its forehead. It was reported to live in India (a belief probably started by sightings of rhinoceroses). By medieval times unicorns were usually portrayed as horses with long, twisted horns.

Cerberus

Cerberus, the monstrous watchdog of the ancient Greek underworld, appears on this dish. He warned of the arrival of new souls and prevented the dead escaping.

Legend has it that when a unicorn dipped its horn to drink, the water, no matter how foul, was purified. This showed that a unicorn horn could make poisonous substances harmless.

The unicorn

Unicorn horns were in great demand, even up to the 17th century, for checking the food of kings and nobles who feared plots against their lives. Most of the "unicorn" horn used had actually begun life as part of a narwhal, a small member of the whale family with a long, spiraling tusk.

Monsters of the Classical world

Ancient Greek legends are full of monsters. Killing one was the regular way for a hero to show his worth. The hero Theseus was not much more than a boy when he faced one of the most savage, the Minotaur. His father, the king of Athens, had to send seven maidens and seven boys to the island of Crete to be fed to this bull-headed monster. When he heard this, Theseus insisted on being one of them. The king of Crete himself thought it a pity to sacrifice such a princely young man and offered to let him be fed to the Minotaur last of all. Theseus refused this, but was helped instead by the king's daughter, Ariadne, who had fallen in love with him. She gave him a ball of thread and told him how to use it to find his way through the maze in which the Minotaur lived. In return he vowed to marry her. However, after killing the monster and escaping the maze, Theseus abandoned Ariadne on an island. According to legend, the wine god Dionysus found her and carried her off to the sky.

Griffin

Theseus and the Minotaur

When the queen of Crete gave birth to the Minotaur, the horrified king imprisoned it in the center of a vast maze. Theseus entered and fought the Minotaur (left). He secretly unrolled thread as he went through the maze. This marked the paths he had taken, so that he could retrace his footsteps to find the exit.

Centaurs

The Greek Sphinx

The Greek sphinx, unlike that of the ancient Egyptians, was female. She had the head of a woman, the body of a lion, and the wings of a bird. She preyed on passers-by in the Theban hills, asking riddles and eating those who answered incorrectly.

These are centaurs (above) —human to the waist and horse below—battling with a lion. Most centaurs were lawless creatures who were uncontrollable if given wine. A few centaurs were noble and gentle. Chiron, the wisest of all, was a foster parent to many heroes.

The creature pictured left is a griffin, taken from a bronze relief of c. 650 BC. It has the body of a lion, the head of an eagle, and powerful wings.

Medusa

Bellerophon and the Chimera

A scene from a terra-cotta relief c. 475 BC. The hero Bellerophon is fighting the Chimera. The chimera had two heads (a lion's and a goat's), its tail was a serpent, and it breathed fire.

The gorgon Medusa was so terrifying that anyone caught in her gaze was turned to stone. Her hair was a mass of snakes, she had wings of gold and bronze claws. The hero Perseus managed to kill her without looking into her deadly eyes. He looked at her reflection in his shield instead.

53

The Cloud Eater

A legend from New Mexico's Zuni people

The Cloud Eater had an enormous mouth and an endless appetite for clouds. Every day he stood on the mountain peak with his mouth wide open and swallowed every cloud that came along. Not one escaped him, so no rain fell upon the land. People could no longer grow their crops and began to starve.

"We must kill Cloud Eater," they said. But no one was brave enough to try. A young boy named Ahaiyuta heard his grandmother lamenting about Cloud Eater. "I shall go to the mountain and kill him," he told her. "If you must go," said his grandmother, "take these four feathers. The red feather will show you the way. The blue feather will let you talk with animals. The yellow feather will make you as small as you wish and the black feather will give you the strength you need."

Ahaiyuta put the red feather in his hair, tucked the others in his belt, and set off. As he went along he noticed a gopher sitting outside its hole. He thrust the blue and the yellow feathers into his hair, so that he could understand the gopher and could slip into its burrow easily. The gopher's tunnel led deep inside the mountain, so close to the Cloud Eater that they could hear him snoring as he slept. "This is the place," said the gopher, and it gnawed through the earth to make a tunnel to the monster.

Cloud Eater

54

Ahaiyuta's feathers

Ahaiyuta put the black feather in his hair, took aim, and sent his arrow speeding down the tunnel, straight into the monster's heart. The Cloud Eater gave a roar that shook the mountain and then was silent forever. When the clouds gathered, rain fell on the land once again.

Ahaiyuta

Mythical birds

Legends from Persia and Arabia

The Simurgh is pictured above on a Persian dish of the 7th or 8th century.

Thunderbird

The North American Thunderbird brings storms and rain while its eyes flash lightning.

Many legendary birds are noble and helpful. Persia is the home of the Simurgh. The Simurgh rescued the baby Prince Zal from the mountains where he had been left to die by his father who thought his unnaturally white hair was a sign of evil.

The Simurgh cared for the baby in her nest with her own young. When he was old enough to go out into the world, she gave him one of her feathers, telling him to light it in times of peril. Zal first lit the feather years later, when he feared his young wife was dying in childbirth. The sky darkened and the Simurgh appeared. She told him that his was no ordinary child.

After the prince's baby boy had been born, the Simurgh healed the mother with special potions. The boy was named Rustam and the Simurgh predicted that he would grow up to become his nation's greatest hero.

Arguably the most famous mythical bird is the phoenix, which was fabled to live in Arabia. It was the only one of its kind and had no mate. Every five hundred years it would build itself a funeral pyre and leap into the flames. From its ashes a new phoenix would arise.

The Phoenix

57

Slaying a dragon

Jormundgand—a Norse myth

In China, the majority of dragons are portrayed as good and kind creatures, but elsewhere dragons are considered to be bad and it is a hero's job to slay them. This is never an easy task, as the Norse thunder god Thor discovered when he tried to kill Jormundgand, the World Serpent.

This long and snakelike dragon lived in the ocean, its body encircling the world. Hot-headed Thor decided to hunt it. He persuaded Hymir the giant to take him fishing. Thor rowed the boat out to the middle of the ocean. Hymir began to tremble, although he was many times the size of Thor, and begged him to turn back. But Thor baited his line with an ox's head and cast it into the water. In the depths, the serpent saw the morsel and gulped it down. The sea rolled and boiled as he thrashed around, but Thor heaved so hard that he pulled the monster's head right out of the water. This was too much for Hymir. He grabbed a sharp knife and hacked Thor's fishing line in two. The serpent escaped and Thor kicked Hymir into the sea in fury.

Jormundgand

Hymir and Thor

58

Marduk

Tiamat

Tiamat—a Babylonian myth

Some myths of ancient Babylon tell of a she-dragon called Tiamat, that existed before the world was made. Tiamat and Apsu were the parents of the first gods, whose descendants began to quarrel. One side killed Apsu and the others provoked Tiamat into avenging him.

Tiamat created an army of serpent-demons and scorpion-men and led them into battle with the hostile gods. The gods were so horrified at the sight of this army that none dared to face it. Even Ea, wisest of them all, was in despair. Only Marduk, the son of Ea, was willing to fight. But before he set off he made the gods swear to obey him as their king forever if he won. Marduk mounted his storm chariot and armed himself with lightning. He took a net, held at the corners by the four winds, and rode to meet Tiamat. He flung the net over her and forced her throat open with a hurricane which raged and swelled inside her. Then with an arrow he split her heart and cut her body in two. He lifted one half up to form the sky and from the other half he made the Earth. This is how the world began and how Marduk became ruler of all things.

Rustam and the dragon

The Persian hero Rustam traveled through Mazdaran, a land full of demons, upon his magnificent horse, Rakhsh. A dragon approached while Rustam slept. Rakhsh pawed the ground to wake his master but the dragon vanished before he opened his eyes. It played this game repeatedly until Rustam grew furious and threatened to cut off his horse's head if it did not let him sleep. At the dragon's next appearance the brave horse attacked it. Rustam heard the monster's roar just in time to behead it and save the faithful Rakhsh from its jaws.

Rustam

Glossary

Aboriginals The first people known to inhabit a land, although it is usually used to refer specifically to the first people of Australia.

Anglo-Saxons The people of England before the Norman Conquest.

Arabia The vast, largely desert peninsula separated from Africa by the Red Sea.

Aztecs The dominant people of central Mexico in the 16th century.

Babylon The capital of the Babylonian empire which flourished in Mesopotamia (modern Iraq).

Celts People living in central and western Europe in ancient Greek and Roman times.

Classical world A name given to the civilization of the ancient Greeks and Romans.

gopher A small burrowing rodent of North and Central America.

Haida A Native American people of the North Pacific coast of America.

Hittites The people of an empire that flourished in Anatolia (in modern Turkey) between c. 1750 and c.1200 BC.

llama A South American relative of the camel. Llama wool can be used for making clothes.

lodge A Native American tent or house.

lyre An ancient Greek stringed instrument like a small harp.

Mandan A Native American people of the Upper Missouri River valley.

mortal All living things are mortal and will eventually die.

mummy A dead body preserved from decay by being dried, filled with spices, and wrapped in bandages.

Nez Perce A Native American people of the Pacific Northwest.

Norse Relating to the Germanic peoples (the ancestors of the Germans, Scandinavians, and English). The myths are called Norse because the earliest written versions of them are in Norwegian.

Oracle A sacred place where a god was believed to answer people's questions, usually through the mouth of a priest or priestess who spoke in a trance.

Polynesian Belonging to a group of widely scattered islands in the central South Pacific ocean.

pyre A pile of wood on which a dead body is burned.

quetzal A bird that lives in central America.

quiver A case for holding arrows.

Red Branch The name of the band of warriors serving King Conor of Ulster.

Sioux A group of related peoples from the plains of central North America.

Slavs A group of peoples who came from Asia into Eastern Europe in ancient times. Their descendants can now be found in Russia, Poland, and other countries of central and eastern Europe.

Tlingit A Native American people of the Pacific Northwest.

Titans The first race of Greek gods, who were defeated by Zeus, ruler of the Olympian gods (so called because they lived on Mount Olympus).

Vishnu One of the greatest gods of the Hindu religion.

Index

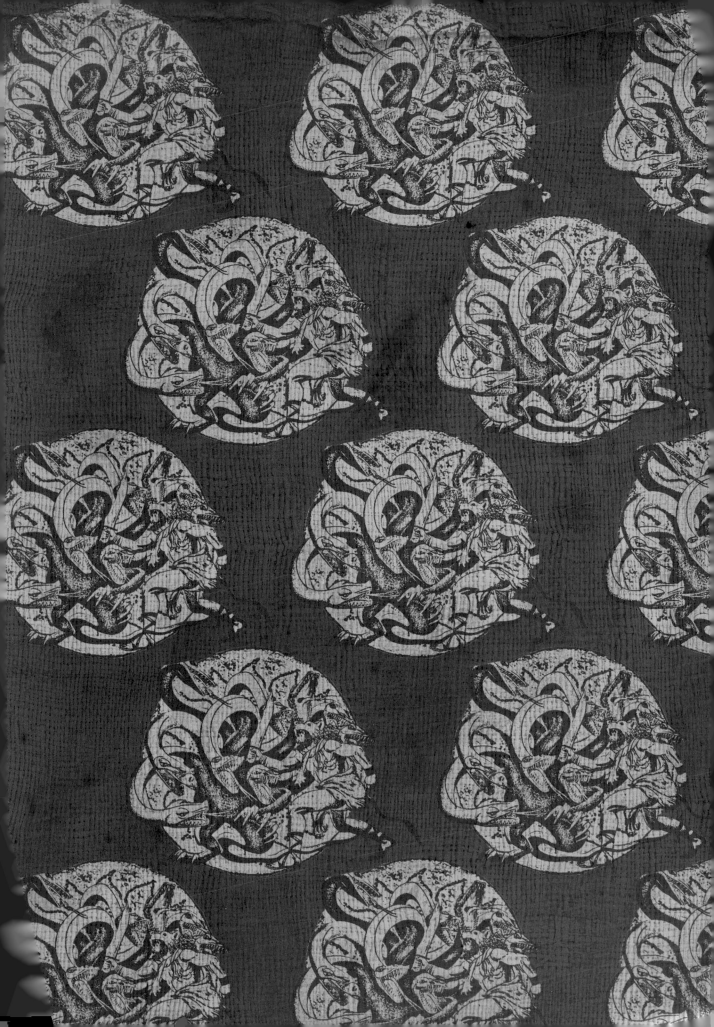

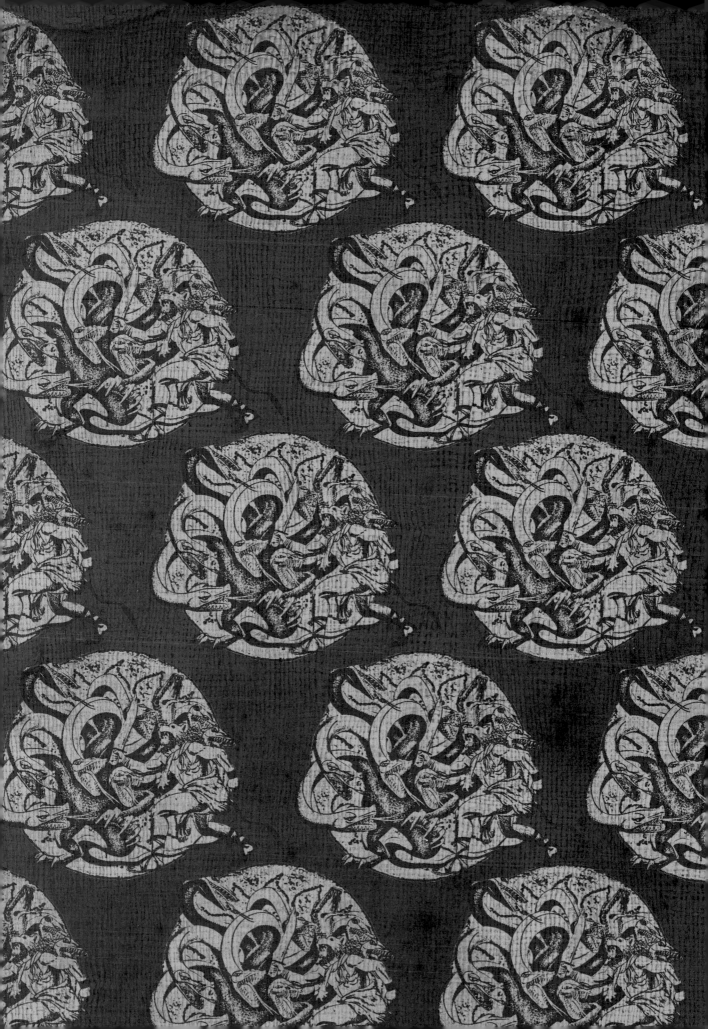